This book belongs to:

....

Old Man of the Sea

Stella Elia
Weberson Santiago

LANTANA
PUBLISHING

Every Sunday, Grandpa would wait
for me in his room, and I would take
my place at the foot of the bed.

There were days when Grandpa
wanted to talk, and days when we
would sit in silence.

One day, Grandpa held my hand and pulled me closer.

"Do you see my face?" he asked me. "Every line on my skin tells the story of my life."

From that day on, Grandpa told stories of the time he spent at sea. He was a great sailor, my grandpa. On board his ship, he studied maps and compasses and navigated the oceans by the stars in the sky.

Whenever he began one of his tales, he would look at me in a way that embarrassed me a little.
"All aboard!" he would yell.

Grandpa spent many months at sea, but it was on land that he met his first love, Europe.

Together they wandered through fairy tale castles and ate picnics in groves of olive trees.

Grandpa loved Europe but he could hear the ocean calling. He filled his luggage with stories and returned to the sea.

Grandpa liked to observe the entire horizon. There, only a thin line separated the dark blue of the sea and the light blue of the sky. He felt an immense peace.

Before long, Grandpa fell in love again, this time with Africa.

Together they danced to the rhythm of drums and climbed sand dunes to watch the sun go down.

Grandpa loved Africa but soon he felt the pull of the ocean. He filled his luggage with stories and returned to the sea.

At night, Grandpa lay on the deck and observed the stars play hide and seek with the clouds. Sleeping under the moonlit sky made him happy.

Time passed and Grandpa met Asia, who quickly conquered his heart.

Together they ate spices that burned their tongues and shared secrets in ancient temples.

Grandpa loved Asia but he could hear the captain calling: "All aboard!". He filled his luggage with stories and returned to the sea.

From his ship, Grandpa spoke to the birds. Whales came and went, following the vessel, and dolphins visited him every day.

At sea, Grandpa didn't feel loneliness.

Months passed and Grandpa met Oceania, and soon love blossomed once more.

Together they listened to the sweet songs of birds and dived in clear waters where fishermen cast their nets.

Grandpa loved Oceania, but before long the ocean waves beckoned. He filled his luggage with stories and returned to the sea.

One calm and quiet evening, Grandpa had a feeling that something was about to change.

A storm rose up that darkened the sky.
The wind started to howl, mixing the
waters into furious waves, and the rain
came tumbling down.

Grandpa was frightened.

The ship reared up and received a blow
that threw him into the water. He told
me that a mermaid dragged him to a small
beach and left him there, unconscious.

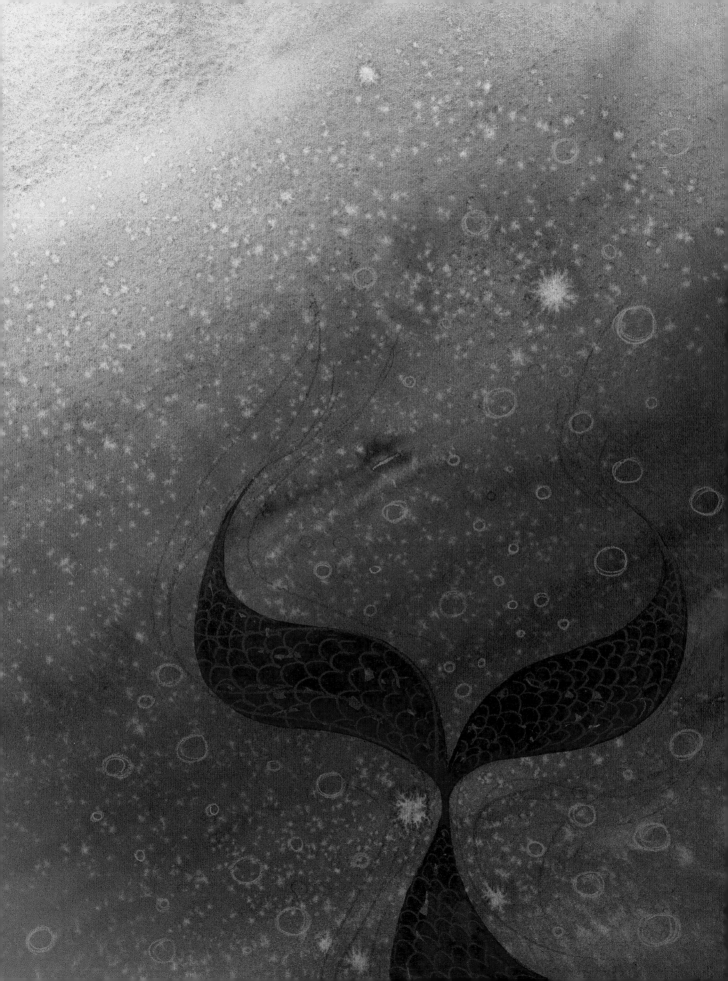

When he opened his eyes, Grandpa found America kneeling beside him.

Together they set out for the wide horizon and passed through springs, summers, autumns and winters side by side.

With America, my grandpa found true love. They married, worked hard, had children and made a family.

For the first time in his life, Grandpa forgot to go back to the sea.

When Grandpa finished telling me his tales, I jumped from the bed like someone disembarking from a long voyage.

On my way home, I wondered if Grandpa was inventing stories just to distract me from noticing how frail he had become.

But I loved hearing Grandpa's stories... even if they were all made up.

Grandpa always told me:

"To learn north, east, south and west, you need to navigate. The land is your grandmother, her stories your stories, and life, my grandson, is a sailor's knot: simple, resistant and easy to untie."

Grandpa was a man of the sea.

To grandparents who enchant childhood,
and to our own Luiz, Yolanda, Manuel and Josefa.
Stella & Weberson

First published in the United Kingdom in 2019 by Lantana Publishing Ltd., London.
www.lantanapublishing.com

American edition published in 2019 by Lantana Publishing Ltd., UK.
info@lantanapublishing.com

Text © Stella Elia 2019
Illustration © Weberson Santiago 2019

Distributed in the United States and Canada by Lerner Publishing Group, Inc.
241 First Avenue North, Minneapolis, MN 55401 U.S.A.
For reading levels and more information, look for this title at www.lernerbooks.com
Cataloging-in-Publication Data Available.

Printed and bound in Europe.
Original artwork created with watercolor on paper, completed digitally.

ISBN: 978-1-911373-54-4
eBook ISBN: 978-1-911373-66-7